GÉHENNE & THÉBAIDES

AUDREY C. E. TRAORÉ

AOS Publishing, 2025

Copyright © 2025

Audrey C. E. Traoré

All rights reserved under International
and Pan-American copyright conventions

ISBN: 978-1-998662-24-1

Cover Design: Chanelle Poupart

Visit AOS Publishing's website:
www.aospublishing.com

TABLE OF CONTENTS

REMERCIEMENTS/ ACKNOWLEDGEMENTS

Pour mon papa et ma maman, ceux qui m'ont enveloppé de leur amour sincère, nourrissant ma confiance même lorsque les ombres m'ont voilé la vue.

À mon petit frère, Marcel, rival intrépide, il m'incite à exceller, suscitant encouragements et défis subtils.

Pour ma petite sœur, Eli, autrement connue sous le nom de Drama Queen, qui peint des sourires sur mon visage dès les premiers jours, avec ses actes moliéresques qui perdurent.

Sans leurs étreintes chaleureuses, sans ces liens d'affection, mes pas n'auraient jamais franchi ces horizons lointains.

For each delicate snowflake that once adorned my sky, only to dissolve upon the touch of my soil. Their ephemeral beauty, a reminder that without them, I would still be ensconced in the shadows, untouched by illuminating beams.

To the Earth, a boundless muse, and to God, the fount of all my inspirations, from whom cascades the essence that nourishes my spirit.

INNER REQUIEMS & HUSHED REQUIESCAT

Even the strongest fire will not
enkindle the void.

WITCH HOUR

As the last bell hisses, you gently coil upon the chamber
door,
Despite the hatred, you ventured inside, an unwelcomed
guest forevermore.
Silent as the specter of some long-lost lore,
Like a phantom, you stole a shard of my soul, deep in the
core.

No mirth remained, no laughter's tender score,
Within that chamber, a desolation, an endless, somber moor.
Your traces slither around, spiteful coils that mark the floor,
Lashed by a crimson thread, pleached heretofore.

Yet, curious it be, your presence brought comfort, a paradox
of yore,
In the shadowed depths of that room, in sorrow's embrace,
we would implore.

MIROIR

Objet tant utilisé, te sens-tu valorisé?
Penses-tu que l'on t'admire, en réalité ignoré?
Personne ne comprend ta véritable essence.
On t'utilise pour briller, sans la moindre clémence.

Pour ton charme, on se fait valoir et miroiter,
Mais personne ne cherche à te connaître, à t'apprécier,
Percevant ta souffrance, ton isolement,
Toi de glace, moi aussi, vivant ce tourment.

Tu observes le monde en mouvement, moi de même,
On dit de toi que tu es une fenêtre sur un monde qui s'aime,
Tu me fascines, aimerais-tu être mon ami, mon confident?
J'ai perdu tous les miens, leurs sourires délassants.

Tu vois, ils me traitaient comme un reflet, sans humanité,
Miroir sans visage, sujétion de leur vanité,
Ton monde et le mien se croisent dans cette dualité,
Miroir solitaire, emprisonné dans son insensibilité.

ISLAND

Upon the desolate isle of existence, time unravels its somber
tales.
A pervasive solitude haunts the shores—an echo of
unfulfilled, fading connections.
Time, relentless sculptor, carves cliffs of forlorn dream.
Resilience falters: uncertain waves, in their rage, crash along
forsaken shores.

Raindrops: haunting sagas on the parchment, an untold
solitude,
A haunting murmur, an emotional tempest lingering in the
perpetual gloom.
The island: a canvas painted with the shadows of missed
connections,
Years drift by—emotional seasons changing; the island's
heart remains shrouded in lonesome hues.

The heartbeat of the island: it yearns for the chilling echo of
shared desolation.
Yet emotional topography resembles untilled soil, barren and
cold,
Drawing nearer to immersion in the abyss of aging solitude.
Time—a silent specter—orchestrating a haunting panorama
of fears in the uncharted abyss.

L'EMBARQUEMENT

Le savaient-ils?
Le savais-je?
Que les eaux seraient si turbulentes, les vagues si menaçantes.

Auraient-ils choisi de m'emporter, de me bercer?
Je trace les lignes de mes desseins sur le pont souillé.
Mes mains crasseuses et grasses d'absurdité révélée.

Lorsque des vagues frappent la coque, mon crâne éclate.
Je navigue sur des eaux hostiles, prêtes à m'engloutir.
Le malaise m'emporte, un cri muet, mon seul compagnon.

Les matelots traversent le pont, piétinant les traces,
l'adornant,
Un barbouillage opaque pour eux.
Je cherche leur regard, mais ne trouve que des abîmes vides.

Mon dessein, remué par les sillages laissés par le capitaine de
ce foutu navire,
Il Se terre dans un coin invisible aux yeux des matelots.
J'en ai marre de cette maudite mer, qu'elle me prenne enfin!

Je m'y jetterais, si seulement je pouvais.

LE GRAND CHÊNE

L'Homme lui dit : « Sois fort, ô grand, majestueux jeune chêne. » « Un jour, tu seras le plus beau du monde, ton potentiel est tel que tu concurrenceras les dieux. »

Sous son épaisse écorce construite année par année afin de survivre dans ce monde spartiate, sa moelle s'assèche, se vide, se fracture. Il se vide de mon essence.

Jeune pousse, il rêvait de plénitude, de folichonnerie. Né dans une terre riche, enrichie par les minéraux de ses ancêtres, ses racines se frelatent dans cet humus hostile. Trop grands et trop vivaces de savoir, ils désaxent certains.

Bambin, il était enivré par la beauté de la Terre et ses secrets. Mais, tel un orage fracassant sans merci un rivage océanique, l'essence humaine arriva et empoisonna ses feuilles.

Il s'est desséché, ne croit plus en l'humain. Lui qui les avait tant aimés, pourquoi lui font-ils cela ?

Vertige lui prit, sa vision se brouille avec ce ciel grisâtre. Son écorce s'endurcit pour prendre la place de son cœur qui disparaît. Ils reviennent, ils essayent de l'abattre, lui donnent des coups quand il s'y attend le moins. Ils le cognent, le talochent et l'étament jusqu'à ce qu'ils sentent qu'il va tomber. Ils arrêtent et prennent son bois, tout ce qu'il y a de bon en lui. Désormais légume, chancelant, il s'indure.

UN ÉCO ET UN LAMPADAIRE

Une femme, assise au pied d'un lampadaire solitaire,
Au cœur de l'hiver glacial, elle compte les heures amères,
Le premier sonne, le silence enveloppe la scène,
Un léger sourire naît sur son visage, doucement serein.

Le deuxième éclate, elle se lève, surprise et frissonnante,
Le vent froid danse, emportant avec lui la neige étincelante,
Le troisième retentit, l'obscurité s'épaissit tout autour,
Silencieuse, la femme avance, laissant derrière elle son cours.

Le quatrième sonne, le cinquième suit avec une cadence
assurée,
La femme s'éloigne, se perdant dans l'horizon démesuré,
Le sixième s'installe, engloutissant peu à peu le crépuscule,
Au milieu de l'hiver, elle devient une silhouette particulière.

Le septième se dévoile, une silhouette apparaît, vague et
incertaine,
La femme court vers elle, un élan d'espoir dans ses veines,
Le huitième surgit, la silhouette se dissout, énigmatique,
La femme épuisée s'effondre, ses forces la quittent,
pathétique.

Le neuvième s'élève, cri du vent mêlé aux pleurs de la femme,
Au pied du lampadaire, la tristesse l'envahit, elle vacille, se
damne,
Le dixième s'éveille, elle se couche, perdue dans l'obscurité,
Le lampadaire vacille, le noir sans pitié l'engloutit.

Le onzième se fond dans la nuit, la femme n'est plus qu'une
ombre,
Le lampadaire s'éteint, emportant avec lui les dernières ombres,
Au milieu de l'hiver, son passage devient flou, imperceptible,
Et, le douzième disparaît, sans bruit, loin du monde audible.

FIRST SNOW

The sky is weeping, a cold breeze wraps its tears.
And pierces my flesh with icy spears.
Snowflakes drift in and out through the air —
Beautiful and fleeting, I smile and stare.

I open my veins and my heart to their grace.
Shining fragments gather; their mysteries peerless.
Stellar crystals yet to be known —
Will I transcend and become their own?

Reaching my fringe, they disappear in limbo.
Foolish me, the transient snow
Does not care about my soul or sin.
I watch it melt along with my longing.

Water floods the land; I don't know what to blame:
The snow that left me all alone,
Or the tears that drown my pain.
In this land, doomed to the eternal first snow.

CHRYSANTHÈME

Malheureuse béatitude, combien je t'envie.
Tes nuances innombrables ourlent un plaisir asservi.
Ô, perfidie, sous ton masque, quel hypocrite dévie!

Un godelureau galant t'escorte, fier et hardi,
Dans les ruelles piteuses, pour sa belle chérie.
Croit-il en la clarté solaire que suggère ta peau engourdie?

Tant d'ardeur me dévore; te voir en teinte de rose,
Sur le seuil de ma porte, où mon jardin se repose.
Ma Terre inhospitalière à ta frêle stature fait affront;
Trop aride, trop froide, elle perd tout aplomb.

Tu te flétrirais, te gèlerais, te briserais dans le vent.
Si seulement il fût un autre monde, un ailleurs mouvant,
Un monde où tu prospères, en multitude de fleurs vaillantes,
Un unique bourgeon, dissipant la peine violette errante.

Trop en demander à une éphémère vision?
Mon monde te dérobera-t-il en s'élevant dans l'insondable
prison?
Ou le cercle de mon cycle, en une sympathie cédée,
Se repaîtra de ton arôme, ta réminiscence rendue?

Une saga d'aspirations, dans le sablier du temps, se reflète,
Cher chrysanthème, tu exhales une grâce si parfaite.

IF I AM

If I am a village, small and distant,
Why does no one tread my cobbled streets?
The windows of the abodes are cracked,
And the well remain untouched.

If I am a desert barren of life,
Why does even a cactus refuse to grow?
The rain avoids me,
And the fauna is incurious of my treasures.

If I am a continent,
Why do I remain undiscovered,
Forgotten by the explorer in their treasure quest?

If I am a planet,
Why am I not the Earth?
Vibrant, welcoming, and teeming with life.

If I am as astray as an asteroid
Why do I navigate with grace avoiding gravitational fields —
Avoiding collision with planets,
Eluding a chance to evolve with a novel home?

If I am a celestial body, ballerina, in the chaos,
Why am I not a star surrounded and caressed by planets?

If I am none of these,
What am I in this infernal dance?
What role do I play?
Is it a monologue?

CŒUR

Coquille vide, en silence brisée,
Coquille vide, à jamais fracassée,
Au cœur de la nuit, sombre et glaciale,
Coquille inerte, tout s'éteint, tout dévale.

Noyau de vie, autrefois vibrant et fort,
Muscle infatigable, désormais à la mort,
Roche de lave, en toi tout s'est éteint,
Au cœur de mes douleurs, il ne reste que le chagrin.

Au cœur de toute chose, tu étais l'essence,
Dans cette nuit éternelle, cruelle absence,
Au cœur de la vie, tu as cessé de battre,
Et dans cette fissure, mon âme se brise, rien ne paraît.

Coquille vide, seule dans le froid,
Coquille vide, tout espoir est noyé,
Au cœur de la nuit, tout s'efface, tout se perd,
Coquille inerte, dans l'oubli, elle se perd.

DEAR ROSE

Tomorrow, the damned sun will crawl from its shroud.
I'll squint through the pain, a fractured shadow, unbowed.
Down desolate streets, where echoes of night's refrain,
I'll stagger and sway, lost in solitude's thorny domain.

As the hours crawl on, I'll embrace the piercing thorns;
Bukowski's whispers and the cryptic notes will be reborn.
He'll unveil the abyss of solitude's elusive thread
In this room's relentless silence, where thoughts remain
unsaid.

Tomorrow, clouds will weep like old drunks,
The wind will howl through the labyrinth it sulks.
My soul adrift— a specter in relentless decay—
Is lost among the enigmatic roses, their thorns in eerie
display.

These phantoms waltz in my Chopin-drenched mind,
Once sirens of passion, now ephemeral, undefined.
I'll raise my glass, dissolving in a wraithlike cry,
For this forsaken rose, its thorns in shadows lie.

I'll sit here alone, as the echoes softly grace
A broken heart's enigma, in the neon's spectral embrace.
Oh, dear music — my solace, my vice, my elusive clutch,
On this Bukowskian night, I've lost the petal of the rose's
gentle touch.

LES ÉCHOS

Je ne crains pas le bruit,
Le vacarme ne me heurte pas,
Je n'essaie pas de les noyer avec la musique.

Ce sont les balles d'échos tirées qui me font saigner,
Souvent, il s'agit de rires lointains,
Parfois, des paroles filtrées par la porte de ma chambre,
Et, rarement, des souvenirs que collecte mon esprit.

Un franc-tireur m'a toujours dans sa mise,
Il attend un sourire, un bonheur avant de laisser partir ses
échos,
Pourtant, je les entends venir, mais je ne peux pas les éviter.
Me réfugier, mais où donc ?
Me cacher, mais pourquoi faire ?

Quand les échos atteignent leur cible,
Je ne saigne pas, je ne rogne pas,
Mais je trépasse

CONSTITUTIONS & WELTANSCHAUUNG

Petits, nous jouons dans la boue. Grands,
le dégout nous empare. Je ne parle pas de boue.

VENOM

Have you ever been consumed by your thoughts?
Fangs where solace used to ought.
Morbid venom poisoning your mind's terrain,
Until you're nauseous, lost in the fog's disdain.

Like Lucifer's hand leading to Hell's abyss,
Expecting scorching flames, but loneliness you kiss.
Unbearable pressure, conquering my veins,
Freedom from the pain, the dissolve of the bane.

But what awaits beyond the swirling mist?
Who knows, who cares, whom to kiss?

GÉHENNE

S'interroger, spéculer, ou vacuité de penser,
Craindre, se lamenter, ou inerte de s'engager,

Vainqueurs, vaincus, ou frileux aux âmes lâches,
Rêveurs enchaînés, captifs d'espaces sans attaches,
Prisonniers de bureaux sombres, sans perspectives,
Leurs songes s'évanouissent, hors de leur compréhension
directive.

Île évanouie, chimère enchanteresse,
Où moqueries et bigoterie dansent avec finesse,
Attendant les rêveurs, prononçant ce doux nom,
Dans ce monde féerique, aux allures d'électron.

Un clone, enchaîné, contemple la clef en sa paume,
Pourtant, prisonnier, des illusions il se pâme,
D'autres clones, affranchis, s'égarent en quête de captivité,
Croyant en leur geôle, prisonniers de leur passivité.

Que faire pour déchaîner ces entraves, s'élever?
Il nous faut des rêveurs, labeur et audace assumés,
Des innovateurs, esprits créateurs émancipés,
Des fervents croyants, porteurs d'horizons insoupçonnés.

Ainsi, libérés de ce joug implacable et pesant,
Les rêveurs bâtiront, leur futur resplendissant,
Dans une gehenne renaissante, délivrée des barrières,
Où les rêves prospèrent, éternellement lumineux, sans
frontières.

BIGOTERIE

Il me nargue ne voyez-vous pas?
Il est tel un enfant, grimaçant devant l'un de ses camarades.
Il tient dans ses longues griffes un objet qui me revient de droit.
Il me nargue ne crois-tu pas?

LAUREL'S CAPTIVITY

In shadows cast, a somber sculpted form,
A figure trapped, by night and art reborn.
Frozen, she stands, as the world whirls outside,
In this sculpted solitude, she bides.

Dreams of warmth, life's vibrant city's throng,
Yet seemingly distant, where she belongs.
Though she appears far from the world's grand scheme,
She is but an arm's length away, or so it seems.

In darkness, stars withhold their shining light,
No moon to share this never-ending night.
But here she stands, her sculpted form at ease;
Once she roamed freely, felt the gentle breeze.

Heard songs of birds, saw the human race's face,
Promised peace and honor in that distant place.
But is this what the sculptor truly did bestow?
A sculpted curse, an artful, frozen flow?

Oh, for her homeland, where she used to reside,
Where purpose thrived and with life she'd stride.
Yet kidnapped, exiled in this foreign sphere,
A statue's voiceless form, she lingers here.

2005

Let me ignite this cigarette, my dear old friend,
As I watch you, the smoke in graceful ascend.
I wonder, how do you endure, I confide,
When I falter, how do you not crumble inside?

Why, when others depart, you stand steadfast and sure,
Reveal your secret, your enduring allure?
Why, when they forsake, do you stay by my side?
Whisper your wisdom, in your silence, confide.

You see, my friend, I've gleaned from your grace,
In your embers, I find solace, a quiet embrace.
You master the art of letting go with no fuss;
With every exhale, you teach me to trust.

Your cigarette seems unceasing, burning without end,
Does it signify you'll stay, my dear old friend?
Oh, dear loneliness, as your perfumes linger in the air,
I'm torn between disgust and pure ease.

CON PHILANTHROPES

Les malheureux de ce monde,
Rejettent l'altruisme profonde.
La vertu humaine, la plus hideuse, seconde,
Où le philanthrope devient synonyme d'autolâtre.

Je fus une élève modèle, dans ma jeunesse,
Cherchant à tout prix à plaire, sans cesse.
J'ai adopté cette doctrine parfaite en apparence,
Laissez-moi fondre, submergée par l'incohérence.

Je n'avais pas saisi la vérité, l'essence.
Que les grands actes de philanthropie,
Puisent dans le cercueil du narcissisme, l'absence.
L'amour, souhaité, non par pure bonté, mais par envie.

CURIOSITY KILLED THE CAT

A saying echoes: Curiosity killed the cat,
Yet it's not felines, but you whom curiosity can devour like that.
It beckons you to explore, seek the world's core,
But in unraveling mysteries, you lose yourself evermore.

You plunge into an abyss, a void without end—
An empty space where illusions blend.
The more you grasp for the superficial, the shallows,
The deeper you fall into these nameless hallows.

But if you let go, surrender to the endless descent,
Soon you'll find solace in the darkness, content.
The fall will transform to a gentle, weightless glide,
In a sea bereft of stars, where the soul's colors reside.

This desolation, a world to shape, to mold,
In its challenging silence, your identity unfolds.
Sleepless nights, like building blocks, stack the hours,
Crafting a beautiful, intricate world of yours.

Yet sanity tugs you back, toward a crowded fray,
Where existence is predefined, and you're led astray.
Filled with people, pleasure, desires unfurled,
And in the real world, you miss the void, your dear old world.

SPIRIT-LIKE HUMANS

Forget the chosen ones, their tales well-trodden,
Known to all, they shine like the midday sun.
I wish to speak of those in darkness sodden,
The forgotten souls, their journeys just begun.

Ghost-like, they wander through life's crowded maze,
In parties, universities, and market aisles,
You glimpse their presence, but they slip away,
Van Gogh, Tesla, Maupertuis, in life, their trials.

How often did they pray to be acknowledged,
Tears shed for their unnoticed toil?
Why must life be for these spirits ravished,
Such a cruel coil?

Yet life made no pledge, no promise fair,
But death, impartial, knew their worth,
In its grasp, they found eternity's lair,
An unending berth.

Life, unjust, in its fleeting day,
Yet death, the judge, would then amend,
Recognizing spirits in its own way,
Their legacy they would eternally send.

PEINTRE ET ARTISTE

Deux toiles, un tableau.
Un peintre, une artiste.
Un bateau, une tour.

Peintre peint sont dessein,
Commence par une étendue bleue infinite,
Qui se dégrade au nord ainsi qu'au Sud.
Il peint son tableau avec grâce inconnue et une volonté grise.
Peint-il un paysage ou bien un portrait,
Sur tons neutres ou couleurs vivaces.
Il imagine ce qu'il peut avoir derrière ce grand pin,
Il se meurt, de peindre sur sa toile, son dessein à portée de
main.

Une artiste voit, de haut, un feuillu.
Des branches au travers de sa tour d'ivoire.
Elle ne voit rien d'autre.
Des feuilles, des branches et un tronc.
Dans sa tour, le vide s'étale et la dévore,
Le vide l'étame, la griffe, la blesse.
Fatiguée, elle imagine un dessein,
Outre derrière le grand pin.

Le peintre donne le dernier coup incomplet de sa toile.
L'artiste n'eux pu entamer son art que le vide l'égorge.

*Peintre attendit patiemment et mourra face à un tableau **incomplet.***

WHAT DO YOU WANT?

Tinted of red, the pages unfold our fate;
Abstract geometries, the law they narrate.
At each fought battle, ink spreads, and
Geometries become sharper and distinct.

In the crimson ink, a question resides,
From whence comes this knowledge, where secrets hide?
Did the authors use their own ink?
Did pages stay intact, why did the ink turn black?

The all-knowers, life's algorithm divine,
Deciphering paths, destinies intertwine.
But ponder, if fire were to claim its might,
Would these red-tinted pages vanish from sight?

For in their vulnerability, strength may lie,
A paradox of power as flames draws nigh.
So consider the essence the fire may test;
Can the red-tinted pages withstand the fiery quest?

PENDULUM

In the dance of the move, an enigma unfolds,
A journey unseen, its story silently told.

First to the right, then a swift turn to the left,
An unpredictable waltz, leaving us bereft.

Its inception, robust, soaring towards the sky;
No bias it showed, happiness or sorrow night.

Yet the hands of time, a relentless force,
Weakening the move, altering its course.

No longer soaring as high as it once did,
But resilient still, refusing to be rigid.

With a new partner in its rhythmic embrace,
Trajectories altered, a dance of grace.

Collisions propel it to newfound heights,
A regular rhythm, disturbance ignites.

Forces anew, a life within the view,
No more roller coasters, just a life to pursue.

Though destined to cease, an inevitable end,
At least, together in the dance, they transcend.

MODERMES

Je maudis les temps modernes,
Les mœurs modernes et leurs querelles vaines,
Quatre murs m'enserrent, témoins silencieux, et m'observent
piteusement.
Face à l'attente absurde d'un signal fantôme,
Devant un deuil qui ne m'appartient pas.
Pour une âme qui ne sait pas.

À chaque vocable d'*Angest*,
Mon esprit vacille, damné du gouffre.
Je contemple cet artéfact du néant,
Kierkegaard face à l'abîme de l'Être,
Sachant pourtant que cette quête est sans fin,
Que ce vide persistent ne sera jamais comblé.

Je suis prisonnière d'un Espoir illusoire,
Cherchant une signification dans la nausée qui m'imprègne.
Comme un pèlerin errant dans un désert sans horizon,
Je poursuis une lueur qui s'éteint avant même d'être vue.
Et dans ce silence impose par les temps modernes,
Je me retrouve face à l'abime de ma propre existence.
Là où l'angoisse devient l'unique vérité,
Et où l'absence de réponse devient seule certitude.

ŒUVRE D'ART AU PLURIEL ET AU SINGULIER

L'artiste, ensorcelé par sa création d'une splendeur unique, la propulsa à travers le monde. Dans la symphonie de la liesse et l'étreinte de l'amour, cette œuvre exceptionnelle promettait accomplissement, succès, et distinction à son créateur. Exposée fièrement dans un musée, elle attira une foule mélodieuse, émerveillée par sa perfection.

Plongé dans la création, l'artiste, envoûté, ne remarqua pas le déclin silencieux de sa première œuvre, brisée par inadvertance. Aveuglé par l'inspiration, il laissa échapper ce triste détail.

Poursuivant son voyage créatif, il donna naissance à un autre chef-d'œuvre, alors qu'un élément de sa première création poursuivait sa nécrose en notes discordantes. L'artiste, agile et ludique, demeura insouciant. Un autre chef-d'œuvre étincela dans une galerie, éclipsant les soucis pour la première création.

Se laissant bercer par le succès apparent, l'artiste ne réalisa la nature profonde de sa création que lorsque celle-ci perdit de son éclat. Une larme de lucidité tomba doucement sur le sol du studio, accompagnée par une mélodie triste. Un écho fit se retourner l'artiste. Face à cette réalité, que fit-il? Il créa un autre chef-d'œuvre, laissant sa créativité s'exprimer possédée par la virtus ou par le vice? L'artiste, aveuglé par sa créativité débordante, préféra ignorer le déclin de sa première création et se plongea avec passion dans la réalisation d'un nouveau chef-d'œuvre.

A LETTER FOR A THIRTY-YEARS-OLD

Dear Old Friend,

Do you remember me?
In the reflection of our past, I owe you apologies.
For in my doubts, I wove shadows on your path,
Placed burdens heavier than you deserved.

Yet, in my youthful ignorance, I tried—
"Tried to decipher the purpose,
Discovered paths and failed to explore those—
with all the timid strength I could muster.

Where are you now?
I hope you stand tall, a beacon of the dreams we once shared.
If only I had the courage to nudge you closer to those stars,
But fear held me, a coward in the shadows,
Terrified of losing what was never truly mine.

Forgive my selfishness,
But I ask you this: do not let me fade,
Keep me in the recesses of your memory,
A reminder of the heart that tried,
And the anguished tears that fell.

Learn from my stumbles, for I believe in you,
You who stand where I could not.

From a past phantom,
To tomorrow's light,

May the pigeon reach you soon,
My not-yet-born future.

YLNR

You are not living it.
You are being fooled.
Stop convincing yourself otherwise.

Their lives are not real—
From the pictures they post
To their scripted personas—
They are selling you a façade.

Let *01111000* go.
Cherish the world, cherish wisdom.
Be curious, not obnoxious.
If you must stand and walk alone,
Then walk boldly—
Loneliness is a gift, not a weakness.

Their algorithms affine your reality,
Transforming your world with con operators.
But I assure you, to them, you are just a product.
Will you accept this spoofery of identities?

You are a human, not a machine.
Tears, laughter, pain, love—
Passion, struggles, dreams—
These are what make a life— a life.

The Earth speaks:
In the arrhythmic caresses of raindrops,
Through the thunder's feral madness,
Through blooming flowers, each a dissonant accord,
And in the frolicsome sun, teasing your skin.

Absorb the world around you and be inspired.
Do not be misled by an illusion of pixel-perfect happiness.

RÊVE OBSOLÈTE

Tel un phénix renaissant des glaces figées,
Je m'exile enfin de l'austérité glacée.
J'ai obtenu la passe pour fuir ces tourments.
Mais mon cœur lié à l'ombre, dans ses châtiments,
Ne sait pas s'adapter à ce monde dévoyé.
Où polluent en vain ces foutriquets noyés.

CATHARSIS
AND WONDERS

*Fragment of glass, shatters into sand, rebirth
as a steadfast rock on an island.*

SHIPWRECK

I always harbored a fear of the water framing me,
Foreordained the August waves to subsume me entirely.
Imbuing my lungs with its adroitness, O, deceitful foe.
Skillfully conquering both my mind and my quintessence.

I am a beleaguered craft, adrift in an ocean of disquiet,
Haunted by visions of my cataclysmic shipwrecks,
Crucified by the prevailing pressure.

But the wind whispers, "Look beyond",
And I glimpse at the endless horizon, as it crystallizes its
gospel.

My ship, forged to navigate the undulating morass,
Cuts through the waters without trepidation.

The waves loom high, threatening to engulf,
But they break— revealing their impetus were not to devour.

As they crash against my hull, I seize the helm.
Steering it with blind and fierce eyes through the water's
tribulations.

A SHORT LIFE

I wish for you a life, not long but bright,
A life of struggles, in which you'll find your light.
Sleepless nights, countless hours you'll brave,
Broken bones from dares, challenges you'll crave.

I'm not cruel, wishing you a lengthy stay;
Instead, a short life lived fully, I convey.
Explore the world, unravel its hidden seams;
Sharpen your mind, don't forget your dreams.

Forge your character, let no doubts arise—
In this short life, let your spirit truly rise.
Open your mind, but never to appease.
Live as you choose, unburdened, at ease.

Live this short life, embracing liberty;
Love whom you wish, let your devotion roam free.
Write, speak your mind, be the master of your fate;
No puppet, but the puppeteer, control your own state.

In this brief existence, pull the strings with grace,
Craft a legacy that's uniquely yours— time won't dare efface.
May your short life be a journey, fierce and free,
A testament to the person you were meant to be.

ADMIRATION

In twilight's glow, the same dapped false paradise unfolds
As birds' croons disturbs my helpless fantasies.
I perch by the cliff, feasting your eyes on.
But distant you remain, in a fleeting fascination.

You seem to be having a good time over there, playing with
hearts.
And what about those eyes of yours?
The way you gaze at them, with such intensity.

You remind me of those candies that explode in your mouth.
Unsophisticated, raw, wild, and free.
You radiate beauty; and by their laughter, their cries, and
their smiles,
I am able to experience your art.

You never look at me, never acknowledge my destitute
existence.
At each thud echoing, I hope our eyes will meet, and I'll plea
to dance.
But I'm just like a ghost to you, aren't I?

I ventured from this cave, chasing a hopeful dream.
You captivate hearts, with grace you sway,
While in this desolation, I wither each day,
Tears leading the way.

I attempted to make myself noticeable.
I attempted to live by stepping outside that little cave.
And I saw you, but you never did, or perhaps you ignored me.

Still, I was amazed by your beauty and by your art everywhere
I went.
The way you enchant the hearts, the way that you dance with
them.
You made my friends happy and careless; why won't you do
the same with me?

I sought to possess you, to be possessed in return,
To feel the fire's warmth inside, to let it fiercely burn.
As day yields to night, my hopes slowly fade,
Nausea and anxiety, alone in the quiet icy shade.

Only warm waterfalls stream down my cheeks.
Whimpers echo like the tics and tocks of a clock,
A draconian reminder of time's relentless scoff.
Telling me the obvious inevitable quietus.

Unlike you, little foe, my face shall form craves—
The water always had this effect on the land.
It longs for lengthy passages,
Reminding us of her destructive strength—
I'm rancorous just by the thought of it.

Blame finds no place, for cave's design is clear,
We were just never meant to be.
Perhaps, in hindsight, a different path was worthier.
Maybe should I have turned right instead, I tell myself.

Dear young love, forever bittersweet, remain.

UNDISCOVERED LAND

Dark, uncharted sea, or realms yet to be found—
Only the bravest or the fools to delve in and astound.
Be patient as they gather courage to explore, embark on a
quest,
With patient hearts, curiosity, and soul's bequest.

For you are not alone, your secrets still concealed,
In spaces untouched by humankind's need to yield.
Keep developing, evolving, in your own sweet time,
Before the world arrives, seeking what's most sublime.

For humankind may steal your soul, treasures rare,
Yet preservation's call, we all must heed and bear.
To keep your essence, beauty, and wonders unimpaired,
In undiscovered realms, our stewardship declared.

THE SCREAMS OF THE WIND

Once I attempted to scream, a fervent cry;
Unsuited to my demeanor, I let it die.
Composed and knowing, they reasoned with disdain.
"Why scream?" they questioned, as if to explain.

My voice silenced, held within my core,
Speaking only when needed, ignored even more—
Invisible, unnoticed, a shadow in the day,
Like the wind's whisper, fading away.

Movements leave traces as I quietly depart,
Like the dusk's fading ray, I play my part.
At night, by the restless sea, I find my domain,
Releasing pent-up emotions I can't restrain.

A potent scream, fervent and bold,
Witnessed by the waves as my story is told.
A few passers-by might discern,
But credit my cries to the waves' eternal churn.

Undeterred, I persist, my heart unshaken,
Though my voice goes unheard, never forsaken;
'Till my throat runs dry, and sounds elude my plea,
The sun may rise, but my voice, within me, shall be.

FINE WINE

I am akin to a refined wine, aged with time.
Every day, I encounter souls resembling a sweet cocktail's chime,
Easy to approach, everyone seeks to taste their allure,
Yet I, at first, exude bitterness, making some unsure.

People approach me with caution, hesitant to begin;
Taking a sip of my essence, they're not always willing.
Some contort their faces as I flow down their throat,
And in their disdain, I'm set aside, becoming a forgotten note.

Left alone in the wine cellar's embrace,
My complexities misunderstood, my flavors misplaced.
But like a well-aged wine, I grow richer with time,
For those who persevere, a taste of depth they'll find.

So, in the realm of flavors, we all have our space—
Some choose sweetness, while others savor the trace,
In a world of tastes, where perceptions vary,
I embrace my bitterness, unshaken by my typicity.

PHOTONS

Nothing can disturb the will of the light.
She flickers between existence and nothingness,
Untamed, intransigent, the cosmos' conundrum.

Refusing to be confined, she chooses her state.
An empress that we shall obey.
Bending when she wishes, illuminating us all.

Charting her path, pursing her dreams,
Defying logic, shattering against the norms.
Her energy flows — a frequency to lionize.

Be like her:
Brilliant in your duality,
Wiggle toward your purpose and against all misgivings.

TO BE A WRITER

I longed to write a poem, but how to begin?
For inside me, a storm rage, deep within.
Empty pages consume both body and soul;
Nightly, I pray for letters to make me whole.

My friends, once close, have drifted away —
In solitude, I bear the pain every day.
If I were to vanish, would anyone see?
Why am I so easily forgotten, as if I'm not meant to be?

THE KILLER VOICE

I recollect the song that you sang exclusively for me. I recall the mellifluous timbre of your voice transmuting silence into emotions hitherto uncharted within my soul. Each note, artfully conjured by your vocal prowess, rivaled the symphony of oceanic waves, the sonorous chirping of the morning avifauna, and the measured cadence of a venerable grandfather clock— the embodiment of time's stillness, enhanced when your voice found their fullest expression.

Your flatteries wove an exquisite melody that reverberated through my being. To me, it resembled the elusive and renowned secret chord, evoking an emotional spectrum oscillating between sheer delight and profound bliss.

You are an adept virtuoso, equally proficient as a singer and an orator, skillfully wielding words like a masterful musician plucking strings on a guitar. You employed your linguistic artistry to ensnare my senses, akin to the mythical Pan and his beguiling flute, enchanting even those who believed themselves to have transcended their youthful innocence.

I had convinced myself that I had outgrown such childish enchantments, yet your tone, your eloquence, and your promises ensnared me. I should have been more discerning, recognizing the artifice in your words, but their allure was too potent, and I yearned to believe them. For the first time, I dared to imagine a chrysanthemum blooming at my doorstep, even though it was never there — you painted an illusion as vivid and charming as the prettiest blossom.

Nonetheless, I am grateful for this artful mirage. Despite my awareness of your cunning yet ultimately cruel nature, I found myself, guarded as I was, following the pan flute's enthralling melody. I continue to indulge in the fantasy of that Asterales adorning my door, for it is through such illusions that my heart finds solace and respite.

EMBERS

Enthroned before the fireplace's fiery splendor,
A living canvas with hues of crimson and tangerine enamors,
The enigmatic dance of flames, a mesmerizing sight,
In this intimate moment, hearts ascend in flight.

The fervent warmth caresses skin with tender care,
The crackling fire weaves tales in the ambient air;
A beatific smile adorns the countenance, a masterpiece so bright,
As photons pirouette, enmeshing artistry with light.

The human, a fervid dancer in this incandescent trance,
Enveloped by a captivating pas de deux, an amorous romance.
Yet beguiled, the hand yearns to clasp the scorching blaze,
Oblivious to life's cunning ploys, the hand obeys.

The mind's voice, imbued with caution's perspicacity,
Admonishes the allure of fire, the hand's audacity;
Yet ensnared by curiosity's enticement pure,
The hand dares closer, impelled by passion's allure.

In this fragile symphony, an epochal struggle is fought
Between desire's fervor and sagacity's wisdom sought,
Alas, too late, the fire's touch vanishes, yielding to the void,
Leaving behind an icy embrace, where warmth once buoyed.

Yet unbeknownst to the consciousness, the cold's aching sting,
Bestowing scars that ache, that linger, and that sing,
The hand and heart both bear the searing brand,
Consequences of choices made wisdom's reprimand.

In the end, no panacea exists to absolve the plight,
As fire and cold, conjoined, form life's paradoxical rite;
The eternal dance perseveres, an inescapable chase,
Where scars, like runes, etch the saga of life's fiery grace.

And though the sojourn may be adorned with wounds and
fray,
The dance persists, weaving an indomitable tapestry. Come
what may,
In the chiaroscuro of rapture and pain,
Life discovers its essence, an opulent refrain.

MY CONFIDANTE, MY SOLACE

Celestial body, as you rise, a fictitious sense of shame fills the outer spaces.
Reflecting, mirroring, the distant surges
Emotional burst of the sun, across the cosmic expanse.
Keep hold of your secret, in your celestial existence.
For the sun's radiance, its luster will evanesce.
One day to perish, its picturesque cataract.
But you shall remain,
True sentinel of the dim firmament—
You will prevail ageless and valiant.

POINCARÉ AUTOMORPHISM

Era:
An expanse of time between rhythmic beats;
In physics, you etched your indelible feats.
Describing the cosmos, so vast and profound,
In patterns and symmetry, your insight was found.

Recurrence, like stars in the boundless sphere—
A universal language we hold dear.
In every corner of this cosmic expanse,
Your legacy endures, an eternal dance.

Within, a place in the vast universe,
Where chaos reigns, a tempest's curse.
No symmetry, era here to persist,
A wild maelstrom in my soul, it exists.

As I probe the depths of this turbulent sea,
Seeking patterns and symmetry within me,
I decompose; hopes shatter and fray,
Patterns lost, chaos keeping turmoil at bay.

STORMY DELIGHT

In the distance, a child's eyes watch the looming storm;
A daunting presence, a tempest's dark and ominous form.
Standing tall, the little one in innocent fascination,
Sirens' eerie melodies evoke their imagination.

Within the fortress, the child's voice trembles with fear
As unyielding bricks guard against the tempest's fierce
veneer.

In solitude, the young heart seeks solace in this haven,
When like a divine decree, lightning streaks across the even.
Obscuring the horizon, it conceals warning signs,
Tales of wonder and awe, the child's innocent designs.

As the light diminishes, the sirens' call unfolds,
The child lowers the veil, where fascination beholds.
In harmony with the flashes, an enchanting ballet,
In rhythm with the lightning, a captivating display.

The innocent child's intuition proves right,
Divine beauty graces its view, shining so bright.
Striking again and again, in a celestial array,
In consonance with the sirens' song, the child's heart sways.

Elegant and lovely, pure happiness fills the air,
But alas, it departs, leaving the child in despair.
In the wake of the tempest's fleeting, joyous mirth,
The child reflects on memories, unaware of their worth.

BRANCHES

The leaf longs for a branch to rest
And the wind keeps singing and dancing.

Caressing the leaf, bringing her to some places
Where she does not belong.

The leaf sees trees full of leaves,
Leaves who found a place to rest, to prosper.

The leaf longs for roots to nourish her green like skin —
Roots to feel full, to fill a semblant of belonging.

The leaf is lost in a blue Thebaid
And she succumbs to this colorful coffin.

Losing her green-like skin, she fades,
She decays, wilting besides her roots' shades.

ZEPHYR

I entrust the wind, for seasons know no loyalty,
To whisk away sentiments in their transient frivolity.
I acknowledge the sun's warmth, an indifferent caress,
As remoteness engulfs the empty spaces, void of tenderness.

I place faith in the moon, in its indifferent nightly gleam,
For company, in the passage of seasons, an empty dream.
Far from prying gazes, from the distant visages,
Absence marks these usual spaces, barren of exchanges.

As seasons perform their relentless masquerade,
They emerge and vanish, like waves in a dispassionate
charade;
They come, they go, with no apology or fanfare,
Much like life's currents, sometimes merciful, oft unfair.

I'll yearn for those fleeting waves, their melody and sea-salted
air,
Yet a bitter certainty lingers, they shall never repair.
In still waters, we both may fleetingly submerge,
The allure and smiles, fading relics, a mournful dirge.

But I'll adapt to swim, as seasons unceasingly churn,
One day, a fresh wave may approach, with a stark concern.
Fear may grip me, as uncertainty orchestrates its tune,
Yet I shall embrace it, even if it heralds an impending
monsoon.

FISHES AND ANIMALS

Women as fishers, casting nets in the sea,
Drawing in hearts with care, setting them free;
With a patient dance and eyes like the tides,
They navigate love, where emotion abides.
Men as hunters, tracking desires in the wild,
Chasing dreams with hope, like a fearless child;
In the forest of life, they seek their prey,
With boldness and strength as they pave their way.

That is what they say…
Bar no net my hands cast, no weapon they wield — where do I stand?

DEAR DEATH

No lover I require,
A promising prospect waits for me, kindling passion's fire.
Glances at me, observes me playing my play.
Wooing with patience revealed and I'm his prey.

Mesmerizing psyche, he doesn't possess a soul, robust might
With power that commands, fairness in every light.

Oh, but I am unworthy, right now.
I am on a journey's long expanse.
Promised love awaits, in daily dreams I drown.

Oh, to be embraced by him, my last testament.
Kissed by fate, immersed in my final torment.
Oh, dear Death, your presence flourishes each day.
I once longed for a Chrysanthemum,
Little did I know that you planted this promised ring within
me.

GOODBYE LETTER

Specter, poltergeist, ethereal tormentor, ministering fiend,
Once a skeptic, oblivious to the ploys you had schemed.
You wove illusions, the deceiving wail of a crying foe,
The architect of shattered tears, cascading in woe.

Invisible incisions mar my fragile being,
A foggy mind, a soul in perpetual fleeing.
Your spectral hands, a vice around my throat,
Tears hostage, poisoned thoughts you gloat.

I sought refuge beyond the grasp of your omniscient claws,
Yet persistently lingering, your essence withdraws.
Invisible, insidious, your presence defied my will,
A denied adversary, a child kept still.

With a stroke of enlightenment, I fall in the light's embrace.
Your faint cloak unraveled, fallen into the earthly space.
This epistle, my final testament to a vanquished plight,
A proclamation of freedom, the end of our spectral fight.

NOTE

Je n'ai jamais été une personne directe qui aime la confrontation. Les mots écrits reflètent tissent une tapisserie de pensées non exprimées. Ils révèlent un monde où les détails, les messages cachés se dressent comme un monument.

J'ai rêvé d'un semblant d'immortalité - écho persistant de ma présence dans l'histoire de l'humanité. Cette collection de mots signifie la fin d'un chapitre de ma courte insignifiante histoire. Une autre histoire, d'un autre humain, qui s'effacera.

Tous ces mots jamais prononcés témoignent d'une autocensure, s'un désir d'exister au-delà de l'éphémère. On rêve tous d'un semblant d'immortalité. D'une preuve qu'on n'est pas si insignifiant.

On n'y peut rien, c'est de notre nature.

Timothée 1:7

For the Spirit God gave us does not make us timid, but gives us power, love and self-discipline.

Car ce n'est pas un esprit de timidité que Dieu nous a donné, mais un esprit de force, d'amour et de sagesse.

9 781999 862241